MW00714012

Best Wishes.

Brenda J. Hodges

AY TUESDAY WEDNESDAY THURSDAY FRIDAY SATURDAY SUNDAY MONDAY TUESDAY WEDNESDAY THURSDAY F

WE APPRECIATE you EVERY DAY.

People who deal with life generously and large-heartedly go on multiplying relationships to the end. A.C. Benson

Good friends are hard to find,
easy to appreciate and impossible
to forget. Pat Larson

It's not what we have in our life but who we have in our life that counts. Unknown

Measure your friends around
the heart. Proverb

Our heart gives thanks for
empty moments given to dreams,
and for thoughtful people who
help those dreams come true.
William S. Braithwaite

Some of the best friendships are those where people expect a great deal of each other, but never have to ask it. Unknown

The best things in life are never rationed. Friendship, loyalty and love. They do not require coupons. George T. Hewitt

WE APPRECIATE YOUR friendship EVERY DAY.

Each time you stand up for an ideal, you send forth a tiny ripple of hope. Robert Kennedy

Nothing is more beautiful or power-
ful than an individual acting out of
his or her conscience, thus helping
to bring the collective conscience
to life. Norman Cousins

Those who are motivated by goals that have deep meaning, by dreams that need completion, and by pure love that needs expression, are those who are truly alive. Unknown

What people say is important, what they do is important, but what they value is most important.
"Building Community"

A hero is someone who has given his or her life to something bigger than himself. Joseph Campbell

WE APPRECIATE YOUR ideals EVERY DAY.

What the heart gives away is never gone. It is kept in the hearts of others. Robin St. John

No person was ever honored
for what he received. Honor has
been the reward for what he gave.
Calvin Coolidge

I must admit that I personally measure success in terms of the contributions an individual makes to her or his fellow human beings.
Margaret Mead

I believe that service—whether it is serving the community or your company or your family or the people you love—is fundamental to what life is about. Dame Anita Roddick

When it comes to doing good things for others, some people will stop at nothing. Dale E. Turner

WE APPRECIATE YOUR contribution EVERY DAY.

What is integrity? It's nothing complicated. It's being a good person, always taking responsibility and showing consideration for the consequences your actions have for others. Howard Ferguson

The most important ingredient
you put into any relationship is
not what you say or what you
do, but what and who you are.
Stephen R. Covey

Few delights can equal the mere presence of one whom we trust utterly. George MacDonald

Wherever and whenever real credibility is established, it's treasured. Ned Desmond

People know what you stand for and what you won't. Unknown

WE APPRECIATE YOUR integrity EVERY DAY.

I believe that the details of our lives will be forgotten by most, but the emotion, the spirit, will linger with those who shared it and be part of them forever. Liv Ullman

Enthusiasm reflects confidence, spreads good spirit, raises morale, arouses loyalty and laughs at adversity…it is beyond price.
Allan Cox

Sincere passion and enthusiasm inspire others and sweep all obstacles away. Pat Covina

Some people personify the desire to live. We are attracted to their spirit. Day after day, they approach life as a great gift, not because of what it gives them, but because of what it enables them to do. Frank Vizzare

That is the simple secret.
Always take your heart to work.
Meryl Streep

WE APPRECIATE YOUR spirit EVERY DAY.

Your good example speaks
twice as loud as good advice.
Kelly Ann Rothaus

Example is leadership.
Albert Schweitzer

By having the courage to be yourself, you put something wonderful in the world that was not there before. Edwin Elliot

Thank you to all those people
in my life who changed it for
the better by a word, a gift,
an example. Pam Brown

Some people make the world
more special just by being in it.
Kelly Ann Rothaus

WE APPRECIATE YOUR example EVERY DAY.

You make others better by being
so good yourself. Hugh R. Hanels

Appreciation is a wonderful thing:
it makes what is excellent in others
belong to us as well. Voltaire

You are here for a purpose.
There is not a duplicate of you in
the whole wide world; there never
has been, there never will be.
You were brought here now to fill
a certain need. Lou Austin

When you do what you do best,
you are helping not only yourself,
but the world. Roger Williams

It brings comfort to have loyal and capable companions in whatever happens. St. John Chrysostom

We get quiet joy from watching anyone who does his job well.
William Feather

Brilliance is hard to describe, but easy to recognize. Dan Zadra

WE APPRECIATE YOUR talent EVERY DAY.

People who invest themselves in being what they can be and, even more importantly, people who invest themselves in helping others be what they can be, are involved in the single most important work on this earth. Eric Hoffer

A true measure of your worth
includes all the benefits others
have gained from your success.
Cullen Hightower

If your actions inspire others to dream more, learn more, do more and become more, you are a leader. John Quincy Adams

There are two types of people—those who come into a room and say, "Well, here I am!" and those who come in and say, "Ah, there you are." Frederick L. Collins

People love and appreciate
others, not just for who they are,
but for how they make us feel.
Irwin Freedman

WE APPRECIATE YOUR inspiration EVERY DAY.

The person we all love and appreciate is the one who's coming in the door when everybody else is going out.
Mason Cooley

When the crunch comes,
people cling to those they know
they can trust—those who are
not detached, but involved.
Admiral James Stockdale

It is time for us all to stand and cheer for the doer, the achiever— the one who recognizes the challenge and does something about it. Vince Lombardi

There are some who live in a dream world, and there are some who face reality; and then there are those who turn one into the other. Douglas Everett

Some people dream of worthy accomplishments, while others stay awake and do them. Unknown

WE APPRECIATE YOUR commitment EVERY DAY.

EVERY DAY YOUR PRESENCE IS A PRESENT TO THE WORLD.

No one accomplishes anything of real consequence entirely on their own. We all have someone special to thank. Here and there in our everyday lives are a sprinkling of caring people who quietly make a difference for everyone else around them—not just now and then, but every day, all the time.

Clearly, it's not "what" we have in our life, but "who" we have in our life that counts. To the friends and family who dream with us. To the employees or colleagues who team with us. To the clients or customers who believe in us. To the suppliers or vendors who achieve with us. To the big-hearted people who volunteer with us. We don't always get a chance to tell you, but we appreciate you every day.

For your gift of contribution and friendship. For your caring and concern. For your loyalty and leadership. For making a difference in the world. Thank you.

We appreciate you every day.

COMPILED BY DAN ZADRA EDITED BY KRISTEL WILLS DESIGNED BY STEVE POTTER

COMPENDIUM™
INCORPORATED

live inspired.

ACKNOWLEDGEMENTS

These quotations were gathered lovingly but unscientifically over several years and/or were contributed by many friends or acquaintances. Some arrived—and survived in our files—on scraps of paper and may therefore be imperfectly worded or attributed. To the authors, contributors and original sources, our thanks, and where appropriate, our apologies. –The Editors

WITH SPECIAL THANKS TO

Jason Aldrich, Gloria Austin, Gerry Baird, Jay Baird, Neil Beaton, Josie Bissett, Laura Boro, Jim and Alyssa Darragh & Family, Jennifer and Matt Ellison & Family, Rob Estes, Michael and Leianne Flynn & Family, Sarah Forster, Jennifer Hurwitz, Heidi Jones, Carol Anne Kennedy, June Martin, Jessica Phoenix and Tom DesLongchamp, Janet Potter & Family, Diane Roger, Kirsten and Garrett Sessions, Clarie Yam and Erik Lee, Kobi and Heidi Yamada & Family, Justi and Tote Yamada & Family, Bob and Val Yamada, Kaz and Kristin Yamada & Family, Tai and Joy Yamada, Anne Zadra, August and Arline Zadra, and Gus and Rosie Zadra.

CREDITS

Compiled by Dan Zadra
Edited by Kristel Wills
Designed by Steve Potter

ISBN: 978-1-932319-61-3

1st Printing. 10K 09 08
Printed in China